CW00842874

For Tim, who likes spiders, and Emily, who doesn't – P.L.

Text copyright © Paeony Lewis 2001
Illustrations copyright © Georgie Birkett 2001
Book copyright © Hodder Wayland 2001

Published in Great Britain in 2001
by Hodder Wayland, an imprint of
Hodder Children's Books

The right of Paeony Lewis to be identified as the author of
this Work and of Georgie Birkett as the illustrator of this Work
has been asserted by them in accordance with the Copyright,
Designs and Patents Act 1988

Cataloguing in Publication Data
Lewis, Paeony
 The Castle Awakes. – (Shooting Stars)
 1. Children's stories
 I. Title
 823.9'14 [J]

ISBN: 0 7502 3305 2

Printed in Hong Kong by Wing King Tong

Hodder Children's Books
A division of Hodder Headline Limited
338 Euston Road, London NW1 3BH

PAEONY LEWIS

The Castle Awakes

Illustrated by Georgie Birkett

HODDER
Wayland

an imprint of Hodder Children's Books

Chapter One

The prince kissed Sleeping Beauty. Her beautiful green eyes fluttered open.

"*Arrrgh!*" she yelled. "Guards! Arrest the strange prince in my room."

"That's a bit mean, Sleeping Beauty," said the prince. "I've killed a dragon and battled through a forest of thorns to wake you with a kiss." He didn't mention he'd almost run away when he'd seen hundreds of spiders scuttling around the castle. Yuck!

"Sorry. The last thing I remember is the Evil Fairy and pricking my finger on a spindle." She yawned and stretched. "Well, I'm awake now, so I'm no longer Sleeping Beauty. I'm Princess Rose again. By the way, how long was I asleep?"

"A hundred years."

"*Arrrgh!*" wailed Princess Rose. "I'm old! I'm ugly!"

"It was magic sleep," said the prince. "You still look sixteen and you're beautiful."

The prince gazed deep into her green eyes. The princess's heart melted.

"Will you marry me?" asked the prince.

"Oh, yes," said Princess Rose. "If I'm a hundred-and-sixteen years old, it's time I got married." She began pulling cobwebs out of her hair.

The prince stepped back rather quickly. "I don't think the spiders have been asleep for a hundred years."

"Too right," whispered a little brown spider called Eric. He was hiding in the princess's hair.

Princess Rose walked over to the window and looked out. Cobwebs hung from the castle walls. Down in the courtyard, the guards, servants and animals were waking up. They were all draped in so many cobwebs, they looked like ghosts.

"What a mess," she said. "The entire castle must be cleaned for our wonderful wedding. Now, let's find Mummy and Daddy."

"The castle's going to be *cleaned?* Oh, no!" squealed Eric.

He jumped down and disappeared through a hole. Eric had to find Otto, the big boss spider. Otto would know what to do.

Chapter Two

All the spiders met in the castle's dungeon.

"We'll be swept away by brooms and dusters," said Eric in a shaky voice. His eight legs wobbled.

"We're *doomed*," moaned three old grey spiders.

"Why didn't we sleep for a hundred years?" asked a baby spider.

"The Evil Fairy likes spiders," explained his mum.

"Quiet!" roared Otto. "We've had this castle to ourselves for a hundred years and we'll have it again." He grinned and his fangs glinted. "We'll chase those pesky humans away! Eric, I'm making you my chief spy."

"Me? Chief spy? Wow!" said Eric. His legs stopped wobbling.

"Well, what are you waiting for?" asked Otto. "Find out what's happening."

Princess Rose led the prince to the golden throne room. The king and queen were stretching their aching bodies. Thrones aren't comfortable places to sleep for a hundred years.

"Mummy and Daddy," said the princess. "I'd like you to meet Prince... Um..." Quickly, she turned to the prince and whispered, "I don't know your name."

The prince bowed. "Greetings.
I am Prince Fearless."

"He saved me. We're going to be
married," said Princess Rose.

"Welcome," said the queen.
"A wedding will be splendid."

"Hold on!" said the king. "*A wedding?*
They hardly know each other."

"Oh, Daddy, don't spoil things.
We spoke for several minutes before
we fell in love," said the princess.

"Your Majesty," said Prince Fearless, bowing again. "In my grandfather's castle hangs a painting of the sleeping beauty, Princess Rose. Long ago, I fell in love with that painting."

The king snorted. "A painting isn't a real person! It doesn't burp when it eats too much pudding. Or pick its nose."

"*Daddy!*" wailed Princess Rose.

Prince Fearless reached for her hand. "I think you have a lovely nose, and I'm sure your burps are very sweet."

The king snorted again. "And what do we know about *you? You may be charming, but are you brave?"

"I'm not called Prince Fearless for nothing." The prince pulled out his sword and waved it around. "Look! That's dragon blood on my sword."

The king leaned forward. "Looks like strawberry jam to me."

"How dare you!" shouted the prince.

"Ah, that's better," said the king. "That's what I want to see. *Courage!* I won't allow my daughter to marry a coward."

"Shall I send out the wedding invitations, then?" asked the queen.

"*Please,*" pleaded Princess Rose.

"I'll decide after we've had a banquet," said the king. "I'm hungry."

All this time, Eric had been hiding under the throne. He scuttled off to report to Otto.

"Tell everyone we'll strike tonight, at the banquet," ordered Otto. "Those pesky humans will soon be gone."

Chapter Three

Music and laughter filled the huge
banquet hall.

"Bring in the food!" ordered the
king.

Twenty servants placed giant trays
on the tables. There was a fanfare of
trumpets as the silver lids were lifted.

The food was covered in spiders.
Hundreds of them. They jumped off
the roast swan, ham, bread, jelly and
apples. They swarmed across the table.

"Sweep them away!" roared the
king. "No spider is going to stop my
first meal for a hundred years!"

20

Brooms brushed across the hall.
Dusters swept the spiders off the
tables.

Twenty minutes later, the banquet
hall was quiet apart from the sound
of munching and slurping.

"What's the matter with Prince
Fearless?" asked the king.

Princess Rose splashed water
on the prince. He spluttered and
opened his eyes.

"Are you all right?" she asked, stroking his hair.

Carefully, the prince looked around the room. He couldn't see any spiders. None at all. "I'm fine," he said. "I must have been hit on the head with a broom."

"You didn't faint with fright, did you?" asked the king, suspiciously. "There'll be no wedding if you're a coward."

"I *never* faint! I've battled a dragon and—"

"Webs away!" came a cry from the rafters of the banquet hall.

Hundreds of spiders whizzed down on threads. They tangled themselves in hair, crawled up noses and tickled ears.

"To the moat!" roared the king.
"Wash them away!"
    Nobody needed persuading...

Prince Fearless crawled out of the water. "I can't take any more spiders!" he wailed, and ran down the path, away from the castle.

"Come back!" cried Princess Rose.

"Guards!" yelled the queen. "Bring back the prince. We have a wedding to arrange."

"Wedding? There'll be no wedding!" roared the king. He staggered out of the moat. "That prince is a coward!"

Chapter Four

"I've had enough of this," said the queen. "Look! There's a fish in your beard."

"*Arrrgh!*" yelled the king "I hate fish! Nasty, scaly, slimy things."

The queen stared hard at the king. "So, are *you* a coward?"

"Of course not! I *just* hate fish."

"My darling Prince Fearless *just* hates spiders," said Princess Rose. "When the castle is clean, everything will be perfect."

"Fish are worse than spiders," muttered the king.

28

"Listen to me," said the queen firmly. "Who else will marry our daughter? She's a hundred-and-sixteen years old! She doesn't know the latest fashions, gossip or dances. She lives in an old castle filled with spiders. Prince Fearless must *really* love her."

"OK," sighed the king. "But this time, remember to invite *everyone* to the wedding."

A week later, Otto called another
meeting in the dungeon.

"So, you all think we're doomed?"
he said, polishing one of his fangs.
The spiders shivered.

"I-I-I kn-know you'll think of
another plan," stuttered Eric.

"Of course," snarled Otto. He waved a leg at a scroll. "Soon, they'll find out that one of their wedding invitations wasn't delivered…"

Chapter Five

Prince Fearless and Princess Rose married, and the wedding party began. Music played, and the happy couple danced around the hall. Everything was perfect until…

… The castle doors crashed open.
"You've done it again!" screeched
an angry voice. "No invitation!"
The music stopped. Everyone froze.

"But we *did* invite you," called the king.

"I wrote the invitation myself," said the queen.

"*Liars!*" yelled the Evil Fairy. "It's just like last time, when you didn't invite me to the christening. Now I'll have to curse you *again*."

A line of spiders watched everything
from high in the rafters.

"Ah-ha!" laughed Otto. "My plan's
working."

"She'll put them all to sleep and
we'll have the castle to ourselves
again," whispered Eric, excitedly.

"Exactly!" said Otto. "Now, watch
while I make sure the Evil Fairy
doesn't forget her sleep curse."

Otto jumped on to the Evil Fairy's blue hair and yelled in her ear, "Hurry up! Put them all to sleep again for a hundred years!"

"Get out of my hair, you itchy spider!" screeched the Evil Fairy.

"Spider?" said Prince Fearless.

"Where?" He backed towards the door.

The Evil Fairy fixed the prince with a red-eyed stare. "So you don't like spiders, eh?"

"I-I-I *love* spiders," said the prince, nervously. "I'm not called Prince Fearless for nothing."

"Then you'll *love* this new curse," she cackled.

Chapter Six

The Evil Fairy waved her magic wand. Foul-smelling green and red smoke filled the room.

"My curse will be broken when Prince Fearless gives Princess Rose a loving kiss," screeched the Evil Fairy.

"That's easy! He *does* love me," said Princess Rose.

"Not any more!" The Evil Fairy screamed with laughter and vanished. Otto was still in her hair, so he vanished, too.

The green and red smoke thickened and sucked the princess into its centre. It whirled around the room and...

"Arrrgh!" yelled Prince Fearless.
"She's turned into a tarantula spider!
I'm married to a spider!" The prince
turned and ran, but the guards
blocked his way out.

"You're staying here until you love her!" ordered the king.

"Go on, dear, kiss her," said the queen gently. She lifted the huge, hairy tarantula spider off the floor and walked towards Prince Fearless.

Green spider eyes stared pleadingly at him. The prince stared back and... he fainted!

Chapter Seven

Many months went by. The king
(who hated fish) put a goldfish bowl
by his throne to show the prince that
anything was possible.

"You don't have to *kiss* your
goldfish," muttered Prince Fearless.

But the prince did try to be brave.
Every day he practised kissing two
paintings, one of Princess Rose and
one of Spider Rose.

Finally, Prince Fearless decided to be really, really brave. He tried to smile at the real Spider Rose, who sat on a heart-shaped web. Then the prince puckered up his lips, leant forward and... fainted!

"Hurrah!" squealed Eric. (He'd fallen in love with Spider Rose, though he was far too shy to tell her.)

But Eric wasn't happy for long. He groaned when he saw Prince Fearless stagger up, gaze deep into Spider Rose's green eyes, and... kiss her!

Eric gave a little heartbroken sob as he watched them walk away, arm in arm. "Maybe if I kiss her, she'll turn back into a spider…" said Eric to himself.

But even *he* couldn't pluck up enough courage to kiss a yucky human!

One thing did cheer Eric up. Princess Rose let the spiders have their own cobweb-filled tower in the castle, which she promised would never be cleaned. Of course, Prince Fearless wouldn't go near it!

And now, perhaps the prince and princess *could* live happily ever after...

Look out for these other titles in the Shooting Stars range:

Cinderella's Wedding by Paeony Lewis
Cinderella loves the prince and the prince loves her.
Planning a wedding should be easy... but not if
Cinderella's ugly sisters, Hiccup and Nosy, have anything
to do with it. Will the prince ever marry the girl of his
dreams?

Arthur the Wizard by Peter Kavanagh
When Arthur finds his grandad's old magic staff, he
wants to learn how to be a wizard. But when he's
kidnapped by the evil duke's henchmen, Arthur finds out
that being a wizard isn't as easy as it looks.

You can buy all these books from your local bookseller,
or order them direct from the publisher. For more
information about Shooting Stars, write to: *The Sales
Department, Hodder Children's Books, a division of Hodder
Headline Limited, 338 Euston Road, London NW1 3BH.*